ADA COMMUNITY LIBRARY
10664 W. VICTORY ROAD
BOISE, ID 83709

D1120090

Cop's Night Before Christmas

Cop's Night Before Christmas

By Officer Michael D. Harrison

Illustrated by David Miles

PELICAN PUBLISHING COMPANY

GRETNA 2010

*To my mother, Vickie Harrison, who has always instilled
in me a spirit of service and giving—M. D. H.*

*To Mom and Dad. Thank you for years of prayer and
your support of my artistic endeavors.—D. M.*

Copyright © 2010
By Michael D. Harrison

Illustrations copyright © 2010
By David Miles
All rights reserved

*The word "Pelican" and the depiction of a pelican
are trademarks of Pelican Publishing Company, Inc.,
and are registered in the U.S. Patent and Trademark Office.*

Library of Congress Cataloging-in-Publication Data

Harrison, Michael D., 1960-
 Cop's night before Christmas / Michael D. Harrison ; illustrated by David Miles.
  p. cm.
 Summary: Scheduled to work on Christmas Eve, a patrol cop is delighted to be relieved
of working his beat by Sergeant Kringle making it possible for the policeman to be with
his family at midnight.
 ISBN 978-1-58980-800-3 (hardcover : alk. paper) 1. Santa Claus—Fiction. [1. Stories
in rhyme. 2. Santa Claus—Fiction. 3. Christmas—Fiction. 4. Police—Fiction.] I. Miles,
David, ill. II. Title.
 PZ8.3.H2434Co 2010
 [E]—dc22

2010009431

Printed in Singapore
Published by Pelican Publishing Company, Inc.
1000 Burmaster Street, Gretna, Louisiana 70053

Cop's Night Before Christmas

On the night before Christmas,
I was feeling quite moody.
Like other cops,
I was reporting for duty.

After roll call and lineup
We all hit the streets,
Officers in uniform
Working our beats.

I answered an alarm
And changed a flat tire,
Then rescued a kitten
Whose situation looked dire.

When a taxi whizzed by
At too great a speed,
I gave him stern warning
He promised to heed.

Snow began falling
As carolers were singing.
A smile crossed my face
At the joy they were bringing.

The spirit of Christmas
Had flooded my car.
I pulled to the curb
And stowed my radar.

Back at our home,
My wife and son both
Were anxious and alone
Because I'd taken an oath.

They'd told me good-bye
And said they felt proud,
But this was Christmas Eve
For crying out loud!

Outside the sky darkened,
And the temperature dropped.
So I called into Central:
"I'm at The Doughnut Shop."

The diner was small,
Open every day, all the time.
If you tasted the coffee,
You might think it a crime.

The dumplings weren't Granny's;
They were tasty but tough.
A man could eat a bowlful
If strong teeth were enough.

So I took off my hat
As I hurried inside.
The aroma was wonderful:
Carbohydrates deep-fried.

My cruiser's arrival
The waitress had seen.
At my regular spot
She'd left coffee with cream.

I talked to the cook
Until nearly eleven,
But it seemed an eternity
'Til I'd get off at seven.

I finished my coffee,
Downed the last sip,
Then returned to patrolling
After leaving a tip.

Stinging my face,
The frigid wind rose.
I reminded myself
To stay on my toes.

When out of the darkness,
My eyes couldn't believe,
Came the fattest old cop
With stripes on his sleeve.

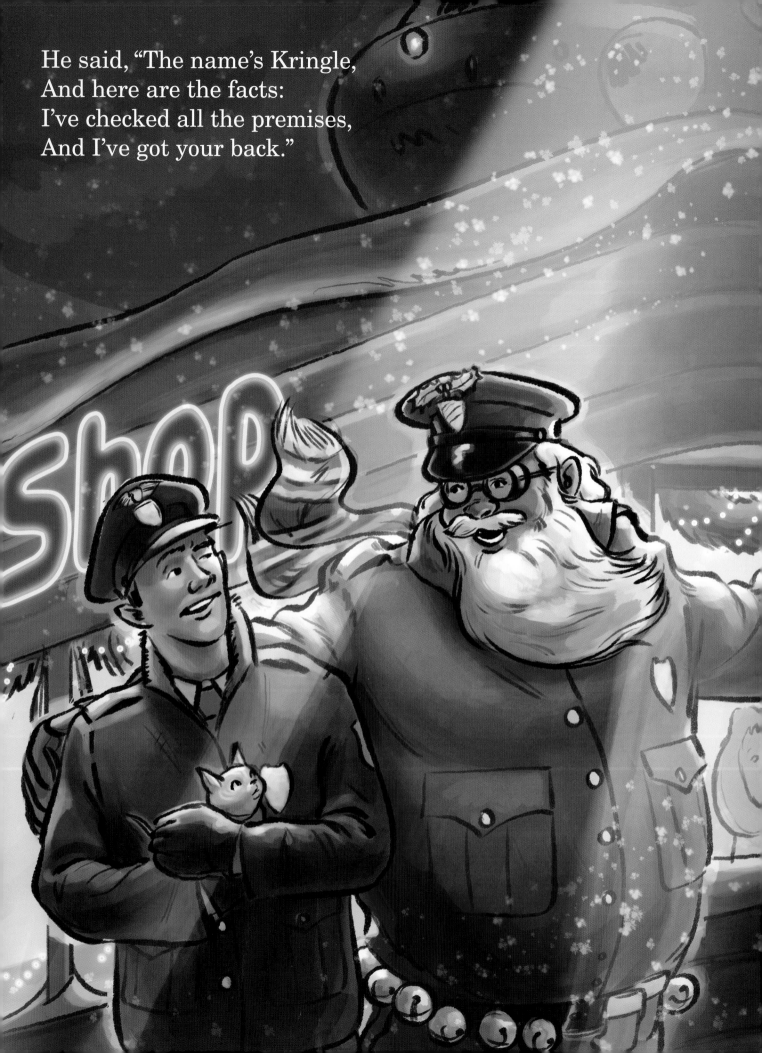

He said, "The name's Kringle,
And here are the facts:
I've checked all the premises,
And I've got your back."

"I may be old
But I've been around.
And year after year
I've been watching this town."

"With a badge on my shirt
And cuffs at my side,
A chopper, and spotlight,
There's no place to hide."

"So go on back home
And hang up your belt.
Sergeant Kringle's on the job,
And he needs no help."

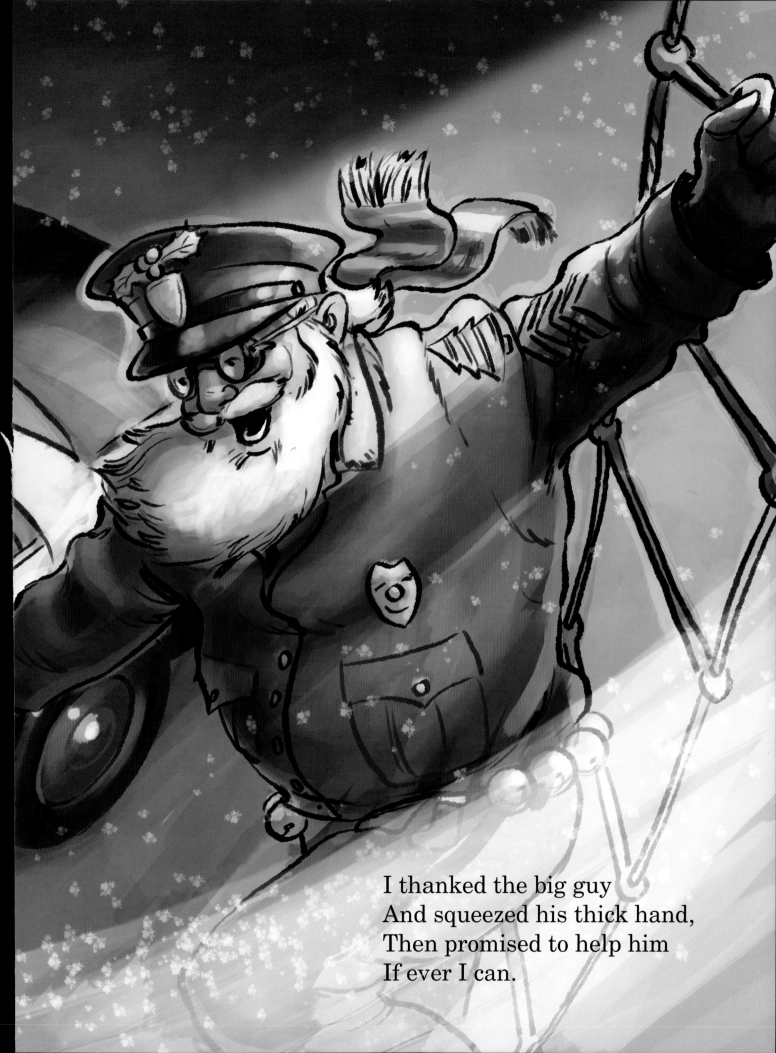

I thanked the big guy
And squeezed his thick hand,
Then promised to help him
If ever I can.

I turned on my blue lights
And let the siren wail;
I didn't even slow down
As I passed by the jail.

Into my driveway
The black and white slid.
I raced into the house
Feeling just like a kid.

I looked in on my son
And held my wife close.
Christmas was now Christmas
With those I love most.

Then, through our back window
Blazed a shaft of bright light
As the whirring of rotors
Shook the still night.

And off in the distance,
With his bird at full tilt,
Waved the fat little man
From his helo's cockpit.

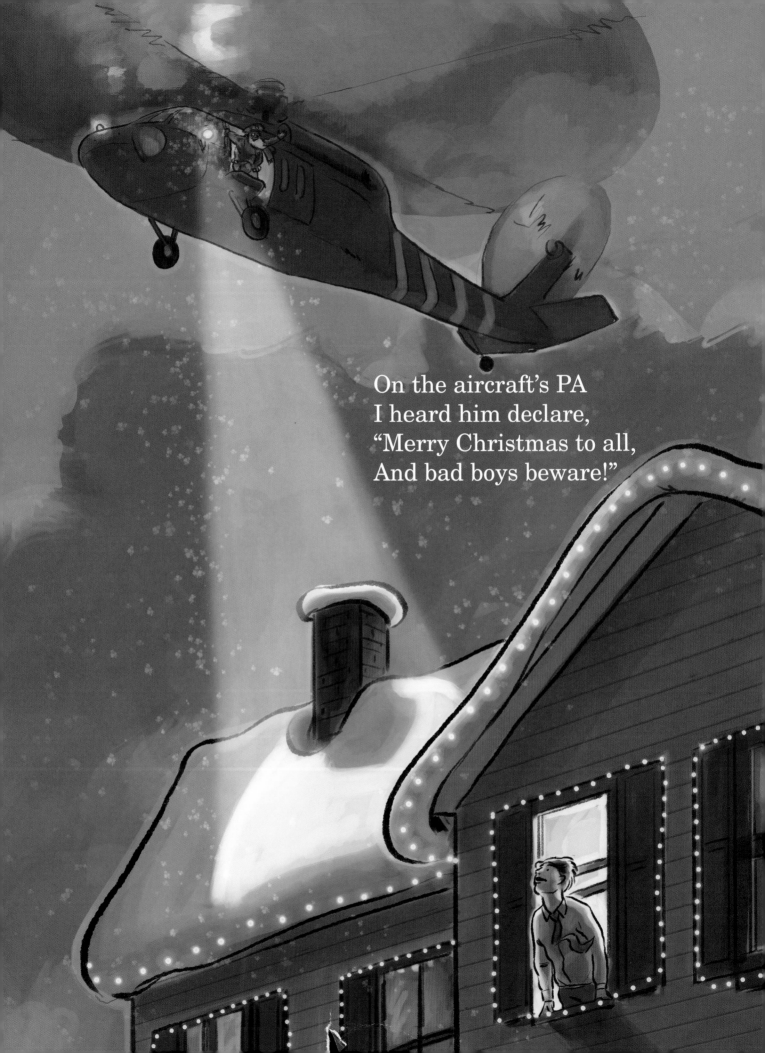

On the aircraft's PA
I heard him declare,
"Merry Christmas to all,
And bad boys beware!"